The Writ

Academy Lea

Rowena Portch

&

Sarah Bailey Martin

Ukiyoto Publishing

[Scan the QR Code and let the Authors see your View]

All global publishing rights are held by

Ukiyoto Publishing

Published in 2019

Content Copyright ©

Rowena Portch & Sarah Bailey Martin

ISBN 978-81-943759-1-3

FROM OUR ACADEMY'S DESK

"Tears are words that need to be written."
- **Paulo Coelho**

Writing is hard, especially when it comes to putting thoughts on paper and communicating effectively. There are so many stories to tell, so many ideas to share and so much learnings to impart when you make your views clear and effective by writing it out.

As we came across thousands of aspiring writers and authors who dream for success in their literary career and want the world to know their story, we formed the Academy under our brand Ukiyoto. The Academy aims to provide each writer and author the much needed learning resources which he or she would require to get the extra edge to take the next leap.

We have created interactive short sessions with TED Ed's "Lessons Worth Sharing" to engage our viewers and impart the essence of writing. From writing tips and strategies to analogies to learnings imparted by renowned authors to motivational speeches in the literary domain, we plan to develop an exhaustive resource centre from which every author would thoroughly benefit. The Academy comprises eminent professionals who are handpicked as our Consultants to offer a gamut of services ranging from coaching aspiring writers to editing and proofreading to book designing and book reading, among others.

The Writer's Bible, the first title of our Academy Resource Centre is designed by two of our professional consultants, who have been in the literary field for more than thirty years. They have helped authors, agents, industry professionals and content developers to produce one of the finest writings and we plan to include insightful references and guides from time to time in our platter. The learning guides are created after thorough research and understanding of the industry needs and provide effective strategic inputs to hone and sharpen the writers' skillsets thus helping them achieve their dreams.

We hope our readers will reap the benefits of learnings shared in this book and utilise them while sailing through their literary career.

Academy

ACKNOWLEDGEMENT

We extend our heartfelt gratitude to Rowena Portch and Sarah Bailey Martin without whose contribution The Writer's Bible would not have been possible. We thank our authors who have brought their rich experience into play and have provided valuable insights which comprise the key components of this book.

We thank TED Ed team for enabling us to create the interactive learning resources for our viewers and providing us a platform at TED's annual event at Hyderabad, India in September, 2019 to announce the launch of the Academy and this book.

Last but not the least, we thank all our authors whose continuous contributions and interactions with us have helped us understand various markets and demographies and hence strategise our published titles accordingly for respective market acceptance.

CONTENTS

Where Does It All Start?

The Writing Game

"Write because you have a story to tell." When I was in high school, this is what my teacher said on our first day. It stuck with me and has kept me writing for over thirty-three years.

The most challenging aspect of writing is getting started. People tend to get caught up on the details. It's like trying to decorate a cake before it is baked. Don't think about the details or try to write a best-seller. In the beginning, your main goal is telling your story—nothing more.

Create a foundation for success. In other words, make your writing something you look forward to every day. Writing is something that comes easier the more you do it. That is why it is important to write every day. No matter what happens, make writing a priority.

There are hundreds of books on creating a manuscript. Practice what works for you and keep an open mind towards what does not work for now, because it may work later on down the line.

Some of your best writings will result when you are not trying to achieve something. Some people need a quiet space to work. I prefer the dulcet hum of a coffee shop. Find a place where you can let your creative juices flow.

Before you begin, however, decide how you intend to keep your work organized. Some people prefer using a pen and paper while some use writing programmes such as Scrivener, by Literature and Latte[1]

It is a very affordable program that works on both a PC and a Mac. I encourage you to check it out, as well as many other writing programs on the market.

Back up your work as nothing is worse than almost completing your masterpiece only to lose it to a faulty drive or some other hardware error. Personally, I prefer Dropbox for all my files. You can access your files from any computer and if your hardware fails, you will not lose your work.

Love what you write, no matter how horrible you think it is. You may not use every word or phrase in your current project, but they may find a place in future ones.

---

[1] www.literatureandlatte.com/scrivener/overview

Writing exercises may seem like a waste of time, but they will strengthen your technique. The following are a few you may employ on the days when you are not feeling creative or motivated to work on your manuscript,

- Write a compelling paragraph that makes the reader want to read more, no matter the subject.

- Describe something you see as if you were writing for a blind person. This will hone your use of senses other than sight.

- Think of a person you know very well. Put them into a tight spot and write them out of it. What do they learn along the way?

- Create a villain that people will love and hate at the same time. This is a good exercise to do when a person makes you angry. Put that emotion to good use.

- Observe people as if they are interviewing for a character role in your novel. How do they act? What are their triggers? Describe their personality based on what they say and do.

Perhaps one of the most important tip to offer is to take other's opinions lightly. Everyone is a critic and their opinions are only that—opinions. If their belief rests well with you, take it to heart. Save all others for future consideration.

You may checkout writing groups and find that they motivate you to improve your craft and forge forward. The right group, however, is hard to find. Smaller groups of five or fewer people are best. Remember though, they all have their opinion on what is right and what is wrong. Do not enable them to define your style. That is your unique signature, it is neither right nor wrong.

Contests are something to consider when your manuscript is complete and polished. Enter only those contests that offer feedback, especially at the beginning of your writing journey. Writer's Digest is a good contest to enter, but it is very competitive. The feedback you receive, however, is exceptional. Writing groups, such as The Colorado Rocky Mountain Fiction Writers, and Romance Writers of America also offer helpful contests and workshops that help you hone your skills.

Do not over-research things, or get too caught up on "Learning how to write." The most effective way to learn how to write is to write every day.

Read many books in the genres that interest you. You may find it particularly helpful to observe how dialog is formatted. You may pick the narrative apart and diagram the turning points. When you read, make notes on what you really like about the writing and what you don't care for. What makes you like the characters? What do you not like? Did the first paragraph grip you? If so, why?

As a fun exercise, try rewriting a new ending for a book you just finished reading. If the book was written in third person, try writing a new ending in first person from a different point of view.

Just as every book must have a beginning, a middle, and an end, each of your scenes must follow that same rule. Does your first paragraph of each scene intrigue your reader and make them want to read more? Does the scene end in such a way that moves the story forward?

Every writer has heard the phrase, "Show, don't tell." What does that even mean? You may wonder. Basically, it means that your writing must demonstrate how a character feels. So, instead of writing, "She was angry." You would demonstrate that anger by writing out what she would do when she is angry. We have one of our lessons covering this particular aspect on "showing" rather than telling.[2]

Her face burned with the color of crimson while her knuckles turned white against the dark steering wheel. The words she wanted to scream pressed against her tight lips. The bastard beside her wouldn't

---

[2] Refer Academy Lesson on Write a Story Not "Tell" A Story at https://www.ukiyoto.com/academy

hear them anyway. They would only make him more intolerable.

The best way to earn your reader's loyalty and appreciation is to invoke their emotions. Make them feel your character's anger, fear, happiness and other reactions. You may love to sit at a coffee shop and observe the people around you. Sometimes, you may eavesdrop on a conversation that makes you feel something inside. Either the people are discussing an issue or one of them is explaining how they feel about a situation. What words do they use? What do they say or do that makes you feel the emotion they feel? Write it down.

Be observant. Just as few artists use paints to express their view of the world, writers use words. Pay attention to how people talk. What is their body language, mannerisms and facial expressions? What typically gets them into trouble? What gets them out? What makes people likeable or intolerable? All of these types of observations will make you a better writer.

Be Efficient, Be Proactive

Enjoy Your Life and Achieve Your Goals

In media, authors—like all artists—are romanticized. They sacrifice everything for their craft, including time, sanity, and valuable relationships.

What makes for an amazing film, however, doesn't make for an amazing life. Most writers are looking to embrace their passion while still maintaining a full-time job, raising their children, being a supportive partner to their significant other, and, yes, even finding time for friends. They aren't sitting in front of their computer from dawn to dusk seven days a week.

Instead, they're writing in their spare time, which for some is just a couple hours a week. Oftentimes, authors feel forced into a tough decision: give up having a life or sacrifice some—or all—of their goals.

Sound familiar?

Unless you've embraced the starving-artist life, it should. I've certainly been there. But it's possible to live a well-rounded and fulfilling life while achieving your goals as an author. It just requires you to write efficiently.

Easier said than done, right? While it certainly is, and it's actually doable. Here are six tips for writing efficiently, whether it's a hobby or your full-time job.

1. Get Things in Order

Rachel Hollis says you should go wash your face. Jordan Peterson says you need to clean your room. Whether or not you're a fan of either of these self-help megastars, their advice drives at something important: taking small, routine steps to create a foundation for your day.

While a clean face and tidy room matter, they're more daily routine than writing routine. When I say get things in order, I mean get ready to write. Set the stage; clear your mind; get into the best possible position for creating. What this looks like is different for everyone.

Given I can't come to your home and whip up the ideal routine for you, it's up to you to decide what you need. For some inspiration, here are few effective steps that may be taken every day before writing,

- Read: It doesn't matter what it is. Whether a few chapters of a novel or your Facebook feed, read every morning shortly after waking up. Try to pick content that matches the voice and tone you need to use when creating your work later that day, just to get into the right headspace for the given project.

- Hydrate: When you feel sleepy and sluggish, you can't write. While caffeine is great, you may find what wakes you up faster and keeps your energy up longer is chugging water. Have a liter of water to get you going, and it works like a charm.

- Move: Work in a fifteen minute session doing something that gets you moving. This may range from yoga to jumping on the trampoline with your kids. Just like with reading, try to pick an activity that you feel puts you in the right headspace for the voice and tone you'll be needing.

- Center: This may sound a little bit too flower-child for you but you may notice that as a writer your intrusive thoughts are what slows you down. Becoming efficient means clearing those thoughts so you can truly focus. A little bit of guided meditation in the morning may help you push out your worries and to-do lists and just write.

- Clean: As is the case with most creatives, they are not the tidiest person in the world. Every morning, take a moment to tidy up your desk space a bit. It may not mean that you get everything perfectly organized and spotless, but move things around so that critical items are in their place.

- Tea: With your desk in order, head over to the tea station and put the kettle on, then pick out which of your teas you want to start the day with. Again, match your selection to the work ahead. If the voice and tone you mean to use is Zen, opt for a relaxing blend. For pumped-up and energetic tone, look for something with a bit of a kick.

- Sound: Finally, the sound of silence might be deafening. So it's critical that you have some noise in the background. Check out instrumental playlists and ambient noise to give you the background you need. As always, match your selection to the task at hand—classical for a calm and wizened tone, instrumental hip-hop when you need to bring the energy, and so on.

With all that done, you're ready to write. In total, it may take you about thirty minutes from start to finish. While that sounds like a lot, getting into the proper headspace can shave hours off your writing time, and that thirty-minute investment pays off.

Keep in mind, you don't need to follow a fixed routine. In fact, you shouldn't. The goal is to find what works for you and stick to it. Consistency is key —just like bedtime routine gets kids into the right mindset for sleep, repeating the steps of your writing routine consistently over time will get you into the right mindset for creating.

2. Don't Baby Your Inner Artist

Part of our cultural romance with artists is this idea that they're delicate flowers who need everything to come together in a perfect storm of inspiration, pain, and drive in order to create. The inner artist must be coddled, allowed to come and go on its own schedule, steering the ship and preventing you from ever taking control.

It isn't that I don't think creativity strikes at certain times and not at others. I do—I've certainly had moments when I sat at my computer and felt nothing, then got a desperate need to create while shopping for groceries. I just don't baby my artist.

When I sit down to write, I write. And you should too, even if the inspiration isn't there, even if those perfect words are just not taking shape in your brain.

The words you write can be revised and edited, perfected over time, or even thrown out if they fail to satisfy you. But, as Jodi Picoult aptly noted: "You can't edit a blank page."

3. Put Writing Into Your Schedule

Of course, none of this is helpful if you never find the time to write.

Actually, there's a problem with that sentence: don't find the time to write. Make the time to write.

Writing needs to be put into your schedule like anything else of importance. If you tell yourself that you'll write when you happen to have the time, you'll never have the time. Life will get in the way, fun opportunities will present themselves, and your ideas will stay in your head instead of filling the page.

Whether you have minutes or hours to devote to your craft, schedule them, and stick to that schedule.

4. Set Your Goals, Then Break Them Down

Yoga is done, the tea is brewed, and you found the perfect ambient sound to play in the background. You take your seat at the computer at your scheduled time and get ready to write. Except, what exactly are you going to write? Which chapter? What topic? How many words?

All these questions are overwhelming and will easily erase all the work you did in getting into the right headspace with your writing routine. Rather than sitting down to write and having to figure things out from there, start every day with a goal in mind.

"But that wasn't part of your routine!" you cry. And you're right—it isn't. That's because we may set our goals well in advance but not every time we may find them. Sometimes these are determined months ahead of time, depending on the size of the piece you are creating, but at the very least, have all your goals established and broken down by Friday evening for the following week.

Much like the routine, what this looks like differs from author to author. My suggestion is you start with what is called an umbrella goal—the big thing you want to achieve. Let's say this is writing a novel. With that goal in mind, break it down into smaller chunks,

- Quick brief

- Plotline

- Character sketches

- Detailed outline

- First drafts of each chapter

- Revisions of each chapter

- Editing in its various forms

- Formatting

You might break your process down into many more or fewer chunks than I did. What your list looks like isn't important, so long as you're breaking down the bigger goal into smaller pieces.

Looking at the items above, some can be done in a few minutes. Others may take many days. The goal is to get everything down into digestible pieces that you can tackle in a single session at your computer. So, your quick brief and plotline might be done in an hour. However, for your character sketches, you might want to keep to one character per day. That detailed outline might best be done in stages too—a rapid, rough outline on day one, then one chapter fleshed out each day until it's complete. As for chapters, maybe tackle them in thousand word chunks rather than as a whole.

Your goal is to strike a balance between feeling so overwhelmed that you shut down and so underwhelmed that you put off the tasks, telling yourself they're easy enough that you can double up tomorrow. Remember: make a schedule and stick to it.

5. Eat the Frog

Sounds gross, I know. However, it's some pretty great advice. As legend has it, Mark Twain once said that if you eat a live frog every morning, the rest of your day will be easy, as eating a still-croaking frog has to be the worst part of your day—or so I hope.

Whether or not dear-old Samuel Clemens ever said such a thing is debatable. What isn't, is the wisdom behind it. Assuming you're interpreting it metaphorically and not actually eating a frog.

When you make your most difficult or least palatable task your last, or even second or third, it makes it too tempting to slow down on the things you have scheduled before it. Just the anxiety of thinking about it looming ahead of you can become crippling. Instead of building towards it and dreading it, just eat the frog.

6. Embrace Technology

Did you gasp when you read that?

It's okay; a lot of authors will. Once again, romanticizing the artist is getting in the way. Just like media never shows us a fine artist working with plastic or 3D imaging programs over oils and charcoal, you're more likely to see an author shown sitting in front of a typewriter than tapping out an idea on a tablet.

If you're refusing to embrace technology because you think it inherently gets between a creator and their craft, let that notion go. Perhaps you work better when writing things out by hand, or the clickity-clack of the typewriter is the ambient noise that fuels you. If that's the case, don't stop doing what works solely because more modern solutions are available. At the same time, don't refuse to try new things just because they remind you more of Blade Runner than the Bard.

From programs like Scrivener that are specifically designed with the creative process in mind to browser add-ons that stop you from browsing when you should be writing, there's a lot that technology can do to make you a more efficient writer. If you want to keep your momentum, chances are there's a product that will make writing easier for you. Becoming more efficient is critical to achieving your goals as an author. However, all the efficiency in the world won't mean much if you aren't delivering top-quality manuscripts. So, what should you keep in mind when it comes to generating quality fiction?

Let's take at look at this, starting with some sage advice from Elmore Leonard.

The To-Do's and Not-to-Do's

The Wisdom of Elmore Leonard, And Why You Should Apply It To Your Writing

When attempting to perfect your craft, it can't hurt to study the greats. Unfortunately, many of history's well-known literary figures weren't interested in passing on their knowledge to the general population. Elmore Leonard, however, was.

Leonard was a prolific author known for crafting gripping crime literature. In 2007, he published his guide, Elmore Leonard's 10 Rules of Writing. While he expands upon these in great detail in the book, his ten rules are as follows,

1. Never open with the weather

2. Avoid prologues

3. Never use a verb other than "said" to carry dialogue

4. Never use an adverb to modify the word "said"

5. Keep your exclamation points under control

6. Never use the words "suddenly" or "all hell broke loose"

7. Use regional dialect sparingly

8. Avoid detailed descriptions of characters

9. Don't go into great detail describing places and things

10. Try to leave out the parts that readers tend to skip

While a writer often believes that rules are meant to be broken, an editor often finds herself wishing the authors she worked with would stick to the rules a little more closely.

With all of the items on this list, you're going to be able to think of an author who broke the rule to great effect, and it's easy to hold them up as an example for why you should be fine breaking the rule yourself. In time, that might be the case, but if you're just starting out or still in the process of mastering the art of writing, these rules are more of a help than a hindrance.

So, let's dive into those ten rules and why you should keep them in mind as you write.

1. Never Open With the Weather

"It was a dark and stormy night."

When Edward Bulwer-Lytton made that the opening line of his novel Paul Clifford, it wasn't yet a cliché. Over the years, it's come to symbolize melodramatic fiction writing and boring opening lines.

In all fairness to Bulwer-Lytton, his opening line has been significantly condensed in our collective memory and is much more effective in the novel itself.

So if it worked for him, why can't it work for you? First is the mere fact that it's a cliché. It's been done so many times that opening with the weather ensures that, right from the start, your audience will—at best—feel like your work is heavily inspired by that of others rather than being its own piece. If you aren't working on a Tarantino script, keep the homage to a minimum and focus on standing on your own.

Second is the fact that setting the scene isn't as important as bringing in people, dialogue, and action. Unless you're writing a script, there's no need to go into detail about the texture of the carpet or the hue of the sky—unless it serves a purpose. Otherwise, the audience is likely to skip ahead to find the interesting stuff—or worse, put your book down and never return to it.

2. Avoid Prologues

This is a hard one for writers to stomach and the reason is as a writer, your brain is filled to the proverbial brim with ideas, and your characters are rich individuals with history you don't want to sacrifice. After all, you're supposed to create well-rounded characters, aren't you?

You are. But having a character be well-rounded doesn't mean delivering all the background information upfront. All too often, writers use prologues as a short-cut for authentic character development. They frontload the motivations, quirks, and history and then dive into the story itself.

Go ahead and write the prologue. Then, take that information and weave it into the rest of the book, finding natural spots to bring forth that key personality trait or reference that game-changing moment in their past. Keep the prologue out of your final draft. Not only will your final product be better for it, but so many authors rely on prologues that if your manuscript lacks one, it will automatically catch the attention of publishers looking for a diamond in the rough.

3. Never Use a Verb Other Than "Said" to Carry Dialogue

All authors want their writing to be dynamic, and repetition is the nail in the coffin of dynamism. So why would someone tell you to stop using other tags to carry your dialogue?

There are a few reasons. The biggest of which is that it's leading your audience and explaining things that shouldn't need to be elaborated on if your work is well written.

"Don't speak to her that way," he admonished.

Why use admonished over said? Yes, he's certainly admonishing someone, but isn't that clear from the words he is speaking? "He said" would work just fine. Or better yet, replace that with something vivid that reinforces the dialogue rather than explaining it. Perhaps his face grows red, or he takes a step towards the other party.

Another reason alternative tags are best avoided is that all too often, they're used wrong. People murmur when they should mumble. They intone when they're merely speaking authoritatively. Authors become so desperate to avoid "said" that they get thesaurus-happy and create confusion.

Whenever possible, avoid tags altogether. Pad dialogue with actions for a more dynamic result. If tags are needed to clarify who is speaking, "said" works just fine—no matter what your teacher told you.

4. Never Use an Adverb to Modify the Word "Said"

The logic behind this one is pretty similar to opting for other tags to avoid said. Adverbs, in general, do little more than lead the audience, forcing writers into the trap of telling over showing. Adverbs with dialogue tags are both leading and result in less-rhythmic writing.

5. Keep Your Exclamation Points Under Control

Writers love alternative punctuation. It's fun and playful, and frankly, it can help keep you awake when you spend too long at the keyboard by breaking you out of the routine.

However, when it comes to your final product, exclamation points and other quirky forms of punctuation should be kept to a minimum.

Leonard maintained that you should not include more than three exclamation points per one lakh words. Personally, I'm willing to play a little looser than that. However, I'm in agreement with the idea behind it. Exclamation points are leading, just like alternative tags. This is especially true when they're used with prose rather than dialogue, as this usage is explicitly telling the audience they're meant to be shocked or afraid rather than just letting them feel what they feel.

In my editing work, I'm coming across more and more reliance on alternative punctuation, especially the exclamation point and ellipsis. Stick to traditional punctuation whenever possible, and don't use alternatives more than once per chapter—hopefully less.

6. Never Use the Words "Suddenly" or "All Hell Broke Loose"

You might be picking up on a theme by now. Once again, we are looking at a rule that's meant to stop you from leading your audience.

If something is suddenly happening in your story, that should be readily apparent to your readers without the word being there to signal it. If something wasn't happening, and then it is, and there's no time lapse in between, your readers will safely assume that it's occurred suddenly.

As for hell breaking loose, that's easy to show with action and dialogue. If you need to clarify for the reader to understand, it's a signal that revision is needed.

7. Use Regional Dialect Sparingly

The way characters speak is critical to their standing on their own as unique people within the story. Otherwise, all the characters will read as just slight variations on each other. However, if one of the ways you're helping them stand on their own is through regional dialect, exercise caution.

Leonard himself excelled at bringing regional dialect into his novels—take a look at any of his works featuring the character Raylan Givens to see what I mean. But something you'll notice is that he did it sparingly, dipping into it often enough that it adds flavor, but not so frequently that apostrophes and unique spellings clutter the page.

When editing, another issue I run into is that authors struggle to maintain this regional dialect. If using it sparingly, that's fine, as it's the goal. What I'm talking about is when a character has spent the last five thousand words dropping their g's, and now they're speaking like an Ivy League graduate. If you choose to rely on regional dialect, you have to follow through without fail, otherwise it reads as inconsistent characterization.

8. Avoid Detailed Descriptions of Characters

If you spend any amount of time online, chances are you've seen people become outraged after an actor is cast in the movie adaptation of a novel. "But she looks nothing like her character!" they cry.

In some cases, this is true; Hollywood executives want a different look, so they go for someone who doesn't match a single descriptor given for the character in the source material. Just as often, though, people aren't objecting because the actor goes against description in the novel, but rather because they don't look like the person they pictured in their heads.

This is a good thing. Readers don't need every last feature of a character mapped out for them. Part of the fun of reading is that you get to create the movie in your head. When the author gets too detailed, they rob you of that experience.

Before you include a physical feature of a character, ask yourself why it matters. Does this reinforce a specific character trait? Does it play a role in the story? If not, leave it out. This goes double for clothing. As a reader and an editor, there are few things I loathe more than an entire paragraph devoted to describing an outfit from the texture and color down to the brand of shoes.

9. Don't Go Into Great Detail Describing Places and Things

Once again, when you go into significant detail describing places and things, you're taking away from the reader, not adding to their experience. As with describing characters, ask yourself why the detail is needed. If it doesn't further the story, play an important role, or at least see the character interacting with it, delete it.

10. Try to Leave Out the Parts That Readers Tend to Skip

In a way, this rule encompasses everything else on this list, because when writing isn't working, people tend to skip ahead. At the same time, it's the most difficult rule to understand as it's so subjective. The parts you tend to skip won't be the same as the ones I do.

To effectively apply this rule, you need to have a solid understanding of your genre and the people who love it. If you feel like you aren't quite there yet, beta readers are your friend. Find those who are big fans of your genre and encourage them to point out anything that reads too dull or that they honestly skipped ahead on.

Adding these rules to the many you already have in your head might seem stressful, but I promise that with time, they will become second nature. On top of that, you might have some rules you've been holding on to that you can safely discard. It's time to check out what your English teacher got wrong.

Lies Your Teacher Told You

The Rules of Writing You Should Break

For most of us, the first writing instruction we ever received was in elementary school. Our teachers taught us the rules of grammar and spelling, and then once we were older, they began to focus on things like sentence placement within a paragraph, varying your words, and effective communication.

Many writers are haunted by the Ghosts of Teachers past. When you write, you may still hear Mrs. Williams, your fifth-grade teacher, telling you cannot start a sentence with "and" or "but" and that contractions are the mark of an uneducated writer.

As you may have noticed, we don't exactly follow this advice and you shouldn't either.

The rules your teachers taught you were important when you were seven, and ten, and fifteen, and you were still learning how to write rather than how to be a writer. They were crutches that helped you get your words out in a coherent manner. But now you're grown, and those crutches are more hindrance than help and there are many rules of writing you should be breaking.

So, what are few "lies" your teachers told you?

Said Is Dead

Walk into any teacher supply store or hop on over to Pinterest and you'll find tons of resources centered around the idea that, "said is dead." Well, as Elmore Leonard would say, this is dead wrong.

It isn't wrong that teachers tell their students this, especially in the younger grades, as they need to help students expand their vocabulary just as much as they need to help them become better writers.

Said is fine. In fact, it's more than fine: it's the gold standard of dialogue tags. Don't let elementary school teachers convince you that you need to fix what isn't broken.

Never End a Sentence With a Preposition

Have you ever stared at a sentence you wrote trying to figure out how you can reword it so that it neither ends in a preposition nor sounds unnatural? Well, you can stop that now.

The rule of not ending a sentence with a preposition isn't part of English grammar. Which might make you wonder how it became ubiquitous enough that it's the one grammar rule everyone seems to actually know. Well, you can blame John Dryden for that. Sort of.

According to Dryden, ending a sentence with a preposition is "not elegant."

Dryden never elaborated on the reasoning behind this statement. However, it likely caught on because, at the time, English was viewed as an inferior language when compared to French and Latin. You can see remnants of this attitude today in how we rank words: "home" is ordinary, plebian, while "domicile" sounds educated and refined. Another remnant of this attitude? Where to place your prepositions?

In Latin, the preposition must always precede the prepositional object. Back in seventeenth-century England, literacy rates were hovering around twenty percent in even the most educated cities. So, a few lovers of Latin (not to be confused with Latin lovers) and Dryden followers wrote English grammar guides that incorporated both rules of the language itself and those of the tongue they considered to be more sophisticated.

Thus, the rule of not ending a sentence with a preposition was born.

The problem? Following this rule results in sentences that don't sound right to the English ear. Take a look at the two sentences below:

- To whom should I deliver the letter?

- Who should I deliver the letter to?

Which one did you read in a stuffy British-esque accent, and which one did you read in your own voice?

This is a problem for all writers, but especially anyone creating fiction. You want readers to hear your characters, not John Dryden. So end your sentences with prepositions. Go ahead; you know you want to.

Write What You Know

This is a rule that sounds pretty reasonable. You don't want to create a book that sounds like you didn't understand what you're writing. However, if we strictly stuck to our lived experiences, the genres of science fiction and fantasy would not exist. Not to mention that the writing process would get pretty boring for you as an author.

Don't be afraid to write what you don't know, as long as you're willing to do the needed research.

However, that research part is essential. For example, you may write a manuscript written by an author in the Philippines that was set in Missouri. At multiple points in the book, the characters would get bored and drive to the beach to spend a few hours surfing or you may write about plastic surgeons perform heart surgery, and private attorneys prosecute people for the state. For all of the above, make sure you do your homework carefully and you have a thorough research to back your writings with data or names of locations and places.

There's nothing wrong with stepping outside your comfort zone. There is something wrong with sacrificing accuracy, especially when the information you need is easy to access. While students might struggle to do the needed research, you can get it done.

Paint a Picture With Words

This may remind you of your eighth-grade English teacher, Miss Bissell. She stands before the class, prepping you for writing a short story. "I want you to give me something vivid. Paint a picture with words."

Her goal is to get a bunch of jaded teenagers to stop and think about their writing rather than just phoning it in. You need to get your head into the story, see it and then get it all out on paper. Again, this is fine in the classroom, but not ideal for a published author.

Think about yourself as a reader. Isn't part of the fun building the universe in your head as you go? When the author tells you what color the chair is, how it feels to sit in it, how high the back goes, how deep the seat is, and where the armrests hit, you have the opportunity to use your imagination stolen from you. And the writing is boring to boot.

Give readers enough to cover anything critical to the story or that the characters interact with in a meaningful way. As for the rest? Leave it up to their imagination.

Never Start a Sentence With "And" or "But" and Avoid Contractions

And now we return to the wisdom of Mrs. Williams.

Mrs. Williams is an intelligent, educated woman. She is a teacher for decades and goes on to become an administrator and even sit on the local school board prior to her retirement. The rules she prepared you for academic writing, where starting sentences with conjunctions and using contractions is frowned upon. No doubt, she saved you from being docked points throughout your academic career.

However, if you don't specialise in academic writing, there's nothing wrong with a friendly, informal tone. This is especially true in fiction unless a more formal approach fits your character.

Now that you are primed on the rules you should and shouldn't follow, you need to start thinking about how to get your ideas on paper, even when it seems impossible. Let's go over ways you can battle writer's block.

Placing Thoughts on Paper

How To Battle Writer's Block

Becoming an efficient writer is important. However, you can't exactly be efficient in your approach if you're struggling to get your thoughts out on paper.

For many authors, this is the hardest part. There are thousands of ideas swimming in their head, and when they're fantasizing about their story, it's vivid, thrilling—surely a novel no reader could possibly put down. Then they sit in front of the computer and go blank!

Nothing!

Just nothing!

Sure, the ideas are still there, but they aren't words and your page needs words. A bunch of them and they can't just be any words—they need to be the right ones.

So you sit, and you think. And think. And think. Before long, those thoughts are crippling, and you have to walk away. You tell yourself it's fine; you can come back to it another day.

And you do, only for the process to repeat.

Sound familiar? With years of experience you may get better at avoiding the freeze and getting your ideas out. So, how do you get your thoughts on paper and battle writer's block?

Stop Making Excuses

If writing isn't your job, it's easy to make excuses to avoid it.

- The house is too noisy.

- The kids won't leave you alone.

- You just don't have the time.

- The right words will come tomorrow.

- The moment isn't right.

Here's the thing: you'll always find a reason not to write if you're looking for one. So stop looking. If there's something that's genuinely preventing you from writing, work on addressing that rather than letting it be an excuse. Make the time, get noise-canceling headphones, teach the kids not to bother you when a certain light is on—find the solution that nullifies the excuse.

Write Something Bad

There are many reasons the writers struggle to make deadlines with their manuscripts. However, the top reason they have is that they just can't find the right words. The idea is there, but they can't bring themselves to type it out if the words aren't perfect. Or they've written and rewritten the same sentence a hundred times and haven't been able to move on because they still aren't happy.

Here's a secret of the most prolific and profitable writers: write something bad.

Now, it doesn't mean turn in something bad or publish a truly awful piece. The idea is not to start and end with something you're unhappy with and others won't enjoy. Instead, it's just to get it out.

Something learnt over the years is whether or not you love the words as they hit the paper, you're still going to go over them, analyze them, overthink them, and change them. If you're going to revise your writing anyhow, it's better to end the overthinking that's paralyzing you and write. Type a sentence, look at it, hate it, but don't erase it—keep moving. Once you finish, go back and think about the idea behind it, then rewrite it so it both honors your intentions and meets your standards.

Identify Your Type of Writer's Block

Never heard of there being different types of writer's block? While we tend to talk about it like it's a specific condition, there are different ways you might experience it. Psychologists Jerome Singer and Michael Barrios researched writer's block throughout the 70s and 80s, eventually identifying four different types of writer's block.

Apathetic Writer's Block

Someone with apathetic writer's block feels like they can't write because they lack a creative spark. This could be in general or specific to a given moment. These individuals tend to place significant emphasis on inspiration and strokes of creativity. More than most, they experience writer's block if they have rules or regulations set by others to guide their writing.

Anger-Driven Writer's Block

Anger-driven writer's block is generally experienced when the writer doesn't want to create anything because they feel like even if they do, they'll never get the level of reward they deserve. When they experience writer's block, they become actively upset and might even lash out at others in their frustration. Their motivation for creating tends to be the recognition or money it can bring them.

Anxiety-Driven Writer's Block

People with anxiety-driven writer's block are highly critical of themselves and their work. These are the writers who'll create the same sentence a hundred times, never happy with the result and never moving forward. They're highly creative but often end up sucking the joy out of the writing process because they're too focused on perfection and not living up to their expectations.

External Writer's Block

This form of writer's block has less to do with the author's motivations and perceptions and more to do with external forces. They might not want their writing to be consumed by others because they don't want it compared to other works or they might allow their environment to distract them from their task. There tends to be a heavy concern about criticism and living up to the expectations of others.

Battle It Strategically

Once you know what type of writer's block you're dealing with—perhaps a combination of several—you need to battle it strategically. Look at the specific symptoms you're experiencing and then ask yourself—what makes sense as a cure?

For example, if you're dealing with apathetic writer's block and you realize this is in response to having rules and regulations placed on the content you create, consider writing your piece and then revising it to meet the standards rather than starting there. If yours is anger-driven, try to focus on a new reward that's easier to guarantee than money or recognition.

While there may not be a cure per se, you can certainly address the symptoms of writer's block and get your thoughts on paper.

Always remember that your writing doesn't have to be perfect straight out of the gate. The revision and editing process ensures that you will have the chance to perfect the way you get your ideas across. And believe it or not, you can handle this process on your own, even if you aren't a grammar nerd.

The Editing Challenge

How to Handle the Editing Process When You Aren't a Grammar Guru

Very few writers are also stellar editors. Even those who are will struggle with editing their own work. At the same time, you don't want to send off an error-riddled document to publishers.

Luckily, there are some strategies that you can implement that will greatly reduce the number of errors in your manuscript, if not eliminate them entirely.

Let it Rest

The first strategy you should implement is to let the manuscript rest. Finish writing and then get away from it for a while—anywhere from a few hours to a few months, depending on your timeline. When you read over your words too soon after writing them, you fill things in for yourself and change others to fit with the idea in your head, missing the errors on the page. Getting distance makes it easier to see where things went wrong.

Read it Aloud

Another great way to stop you from correcting mistakes in your head and missing them on the page is to read the manuscript aloud to yourself. It's going to be time-consuming but the results are worth it.

If you're comfortable with embracing technology, there are ways to make this step easier on you such as having a text-to-voice program, like Word Talk, read it to you. So long as the robotic voice and sometimes unusual pronunciation don't throw you off, you should be able to spot errors with your ears that you can't pick up with your eyes.

Identify the Words and Phrases You Rely On

As you go over your manuscript, look for crutch words and phrases—those that you repeat far too often in your writing. Once you spot them, it can be a bit embarrassing, but don't feel ashamed: we all have them. In some cases, they can even pop up as a result of trying to make your writing more dynamic.

For example, an author who wanted to get away from "typical" action words ended up using "slid" over sixty times in her manuscript. Keep in mind that once you identify your crutch words and phrases, you don't need to eliminate them; just try to change things up more often. It can be helpful to have a master list of alternatives that you can rely on while revising.

Use the Right Tools

There are so many tools you can run your writing through to make it easier to analyze it. Grammarly is one that's always mentioned, and it's undoubtedly one of the best grammar checkers on the market. For spelling, Word's built-in spellcheck still does a great job. ProWritingAid is another checker that many authors rely on, and it comes with some unique checks that allow you to target specific issues, such as homophone confusion.

To find words and phrases you're repeating, use a keyword analyzer; while these are meant for SEO analysis, they'll still tell you exactly how many times you used words and phrases, and most will ignore words like "and," "but," "he," and "she." You may need to analyze your manuscript in sections, but the time it takes is worth the results you get.

Hemingway App helps you see if you're varying your sentence structure enough. You can also use readability checkers to make sure your content is written for the literacy level of your target audience—great for people who write for children and teens. Chances are good that whatever writing traps you struggle with, there are tools that can help you target them and improve.

Exchange With A Writing Partner

On Facebook and other platforms, there are numerous writing communities where aspiring authors get together and exchange files for editing and critiquing. If you really struggle with critically analyzing your own work, this can be an ideal way to discover what you need to change about your book. Additionally, the process of critiquing another writer can help you give a more critical eye to your manuscript.

Collaborate With Savvy Beta Readers

Beta readers are a critical part of the publishing process. These readers go over your manuscript for free or a meager fee and give you feedback on it. Sometimes, this is just a general response to the piece as a whole, while others will point out errors and reactions line by line. If you find the right beta readers, it's a good idea to form a strong relationship with them, as they could become key to your manuscript being published.

Hire A Professional

For many authors, writing is more a hobby than a business, and that can make shelling out for a professional editor a painful prospect. Given that some editors will charge thousands of dollars to review a standard novel-length manuscript, I understand this hesitation. Keep in mind that not every editor will charge prices that break the bank and that different levels of editing are cheaper than others. The more you can handle yourself, the lower the fee.

By the time you are done editing, you will have come a long way in your journey as a writer. However, it isn't quite done. Now it is time to tackle the publishing process.

What Goes Into Producing A Book?

When you first start out, you might be tempted to do your own thing. I highly suggest that you practice what has been proven for many successful authors. It will save you time in the end.

Observe and practice the seven basic stages of writing,

1. Prewriting

2. Researching

3. Writing the Draft

4. Revising

5. Editing and Proofreading

6. Typesetting and Formatting

7. Quality Check

1. Prewriting

Take your idea and flush it out. What is the main theme of the story or manuscript? The theme should be explained in one concise statement. For example,

Fiction: A woman finds a dead man in her home, clinging to a love letter she had written ten years ago.

Non-Fiction: A blind woman's journey from sight to blindness.

Who is your audience and what will they expect to gain from reading your work?

Answer the questions, who, what, why, how, and when for every character in your story. Interview each of your characters until you have a clear image of who they are and why they do what they do. I like to start with a person I know and put her into a situation she would find particularly challenging. For example, I have a friend who is terrified of heights. Naturally, I created a scene where she has to climb a very tall tree to save a child.

For each character, describe their normal everyday life. What is the one thing he or she wants the most? What happens in their life that prevents them from achieving their goal? How do they overcome those challenges? How do they change as a person by overcoming the obstacles? Do they ever achieve their original goal, or did another goal replace that desire?

Write a backstory for each of your characters that explain why they think, feel, or behave as they do. Who are the people close to them? Who do they despise and why?

This may seem like a lot of work, but it will help your characters come to life.

I find it helpful to create a basic narrative outline so that I have a goal and clear direction. I tend to write the beginning, middle, and end summaries. There are hundreds of books on outlining. Find a method that works for you.

If you want to bounce your narrative outline off people, this is the stage in which to do it. Tell your basic storyline and see if it works. The more you tell your story verbally, the easier it is to work out the narrative kinks.

Do not start writing without performing the prewriting steps, or the last two steps will become quite daunting, I assure you. The more work you put into the prewriting stage, the easier your manuscript will come together.

2. Researching

Do your research. Make sure you are writing something your audience will believe. One mistake could turn a fan into a disgruntled non-believer of your work.

Know the scenery among which your characters live. When you describe a place, your readers want to feel as if they are there, experiencing what your characters see, touch, smell, and hear.

For your first manuscript, it is best to start with what you know. Write about an area you are familiar with and places you frequent.

Do not write about something you know little about. Your audience will know and will lose faith in you.

3. Writing The Draft

Have fun with this stage. It is the main stage where you can write with complete abandon.

This is the perhaps the most exciting stage of writing. This is where your story begins, continues, and ends. It reaches the infancy stage, where it learns to walk, talk, and explore options. Your characters will come to life, and may surprise you. You may often get frustrated with your characters when they decide to go a complete opposite direction from what you had intended. In truth, however, the characters' decisions are typically the right choice. You may just go along with it, cursing them under your breath and write them into the sticky wicket they are so determined to enter.

Allow your creativity to flow during this stage. Don't worry if a scene is not turning out the way you expect. Keep writing, you can edit it later during the revision stage. Just remember that every word you write is important, even if it is cut out later, it might hold a gem of matter in the end.

You do not have to write a book in sequential order. You may write a particular scene completely out of sequence because it is fresh in your mind and you are in the mood to write it. Sometimes, you feel a bit more emotional. This is when you write scenes designed to play on the reader's heart strings. You may write your best emotional scenes when you are feeling depressed. Use your own emotions and state of mind to propel you forward. When you're angry, you may try out writing a villain scene. When you're feeling witty and sharp, you may write your best dialog. Be creative and open to write whatever feels natural. You can easily slide the scenes in place when you are ready.

You may try to write a draft of a sixty thousand word story in about two months. The quicker, the better. You can easily do this by writing for only one hour per day. If you are most creative in the morning, wake up an hour early and get to writing before the bustle of your day begins. Set your boundaries and hold them lest others determine them for you. Writing is important. Make sure your family understands that fact.

If you need good motivation for writing fifty thousand words in one month, it is highly suggested you join NaNoWriMo every November.[3]

Do not go back and rewrite anything during the draft stage. The entire idea of writing the draft is getting it down in words. If you continue to rewrite, you will lose your momentum and your narrative flow will be compromised.

Do not allow anyone to read your draft for any reason. The story is not done. People love to offer feedback. During this stage, that feedback can be detrimental, discouraging, and may halt your progress.

4. Revising

Revise with your focus on the narrative plot.

The goal of revision is to remain focused on a particular aspect of your story. In this stage of revision, you are not necessarily looking for grammatical errors or sentence structure.

---

[3] Visit their site for more information: www.nanowrimo.org.

Read your story through as if you are a casual reader. Make notes in the areas that don't work, or that don't drive the narrative plot forward. Look for redundancies and holes. Try not to correct these issues straight away. Just keep reading and making notes until you reach the end of your story.

Correct the issues you noted during your first revision pass, and then read through the story again. This time, concentrate on inconsistencies. You don't want to describe your character with blue eyes, only to have them turn brown during a scene. Again, make notes, and continue reading.

Correct the inconsistencies you noted. Read through the story again, this time concentrating on each scene. Does the first paragraph grab your attention? Does the end of the scene make you want to read more? Does the scene drive the plot forward or does it stall the flow?

Correct the areas that need help. Read through your manuscript again, this time focusing on dialog. Does each character have a unique voice? Does the dialog flow naturally? Do you know who is talking? Are you over-using the "he said," or "she said" tag? There are several good books on creating good dialog. If this is a struggle for you, do a bit of studying on this writing aspect.

Do not try to read through once during the revision stage and focus on all aspects of revision. You will miss something.

Do not take the time to fix errors as you see them. Make a note of the error and move on. You want to maintain the continuity of continuous reading. Some errors will take time and thought to correct. It is best to just make a note of them and continue on.

5. Editing and Proofreading

This is the most important stage of creating a finished manuscript.

Editing consists of correcting grammar and sentence structure. If you are not comfortable in this area, it is highly suggested to invest in an editing program, such as Grammarly or ProWriting Aid. These programs will flag common grammatical errors and style issues and they are definitely worth the cost.

After making your corrections, read your entire manuscript aloud. This may sound odd, but you will catch many more errors by doing this. Reading aloud uses a different part of your brain that is not so willing to forgive simple errors that your subconscious may overlook. You will also get a feel for the flow of your writing. What works when reading silently may sound awkward when read aloud. You may try recording your readings so that you can listen to them again with a different frame of mind.

Make your corrections. Now, it is time to let your manuscript rest. Do not look at it again for at least one full week.

Read your manuscript again and correct any additional errors. If at all possible, find a professional editor to proofread your document. Proofreading costs much less than line editing. Most editors will read a few chapters and will let you know which type of service they recommend.

If you are fortunate to have some friends who are particularly good at editing, you may exchange for their help, by contributing to their blogs or edit their material. Editing your own work is not recommended. Even professional editors do not edit their own material as they are so close to it.

Do not skimp on the editing stage. Paying for a professional edit can make your manuscript shine.

6. Typesetting and Formatting

Typesetting is the process of formatting your book's interior for printing or ebook publication.

It is possible to typeset your book in Word, however, it is not recommended and it will appear unprofessional to those who can spot the difference. Word files can also be a bit unpredictable when vetted for printing.

Most professionals use Adobe InDesign for typesetting, but there are several, more affordable options on the market as well.

The typesetting is followed by print and eBook formatting.

The book format should make it a pleasant reading experience for the reader. The page layout should be clean and unobtrusive. Placement of the page numbers, title, and author's name should appear consistent throughout the book.

If your book is a non-fiction book, chapters can start on either an odd or even page, depending on where the previous chapter ends. In other words, it can be contiguous without any blank pages.

If your book is fiction, new chapters start on the next odd page. For example, if the previous chapter ends on page 7, page 8 will be blank and the next chapter will start on page 9. This is not a hard rule of thumb, but it is typical in the publishing industry.

The first page of a chapter typically begins a third of the way down the page.

For placing matter in the front and the back of your storyline

Front matter contains your title page, imprint and copyright information, and acknowledgments if applicable. Front matter uses roman numerals for page numbers.

Back matter may contain a more in-depth author bio, a sample chapter from another book, a list of other books written by the author, an index or appendix, or other type of information.

Back matter is a good place to put information that may entice your readers to purchase more of your books. I highly recommend including one to three sample chapters from your next book. You can also include a link to where your books are sold, or to your author website.

Next comes the eBook formatting which is an art best practiced by professionals who know what they are doing. There are many types of ebook readers on the market. Your finished eBook file may look great with one type of reader, but horrible on another type of reader.

Scrivener does a good job at producing consistent formats, but they are simple, at best. I am a Mac user, so I use iBooks Author to produce my eBook content.

If you intend on publishing through a service, such as Smashwords, make sure you read through their publishing guidelines. Most of the time, they require a Word file that meets particular formatting standards. The nice thing about publishing through Smashwords is that they produce all the various forms of eBooks for you, providing your Word file is formatted correctly.

The final and one of the most important part comes with designing the Cover.

Book covers are the first thing a potential reader sees. A simple glimpse of a thumbnail image is all you have to attract a reader's attention. Out of hundreds of book images, what will make yours stand out?

If you are not savvy with digital illustration programs, such as Adobe Photoshop, Illustrator, and the likes, I highly suggest you get a professional to design a cover for you. There are several specifications you must consider when designing a cover:

- An image design that accurately depicts your book genre and theme

- Back cover matter (blurb, bio, imprint)

- Book dimensions

- Barcode location

- Font

- Spine width

- Bleed margins

Creating an image design that accurately depicts your book genre and theme

Take a look at the books on Amazon to get an idea of what other books in your genre look like. Focus only on the best sellers. Make a note of what you like and don't like about each one. Which ones caught your eye first? Why? Which ones intrigued your interest to read the book? Why?

Based on what you found, you should have an idea of what will work for your book. Think about what will make your book cover stand out above the others. For example, if most of the books use dark colors, think about using lighter ones. If most books use photos on the front cover, think about using an illustration.

Most importantly, your image should reflect the theme you wrote during the prewriting stage.

Create your book cover image at 300dpi to preserve clarity and focus. Anything less may cause your image to appear blurry when printed. Note the following parameters while designing your Cover,

a. Back Cover Matter (blurb, bio, imprint)

Your book blurb is not a synopsis. It is a quick recap of the storyline. Readers will use this blurb to determine whether or not your book is worth investing in. One to two short paragraphs should be enough to hook your reader into purchasing your book.

I like to write several versions and put them out on Facebook to get feedback. You would be surprised at how well this works. Set it up so that your followers can vote on which blurb they like best.

Your bio should recap who you are and intrigue your audience. Make sure you include what makes you unique, necessary credentials, and something interesting about your personality. Keep it brief and concise.

b. Endorsements

Connect with other authors in your genre and ask them for an endorsement to add to the back of your cover. This is not required, but it does give your book credibility.

c. Book dimensions

Your book cover must meet dimension specifications based on the print copy size of your book. Each printer has their own set of specifications. Amazon KDP (Kindle Direct Publishing)[4] is a good standard to follow.

If your book cover dimensions do not meet your printer's specifications, it might fail the pre-flight check and you will have to make adjustments. It is much easier to get it right the first time.

d. Barcode Location

The standard barcode specifications are as follows,

- 2" (50.8 mm) wide and 1.2" (30.5 mm) tall

- At least .25" (6 mm) from the cover's edge

- Vector images are preferred

- At least 300 dots per inch if the barcode is rasterized

- Solid white background

- Barcode is 100% black (no colors or registration black)

---

[4] https://kdp.amazon.com/en_US/help/topic/G201857950

- Right-side up and square to the cover

- Not flattened into main cover as one single image

e. Font

As a general rule of thumb, you do not want to incorporate more than two different fonts on your cover.

Choose a font that is easy to read. If your potential readers cannot read the book title or blurb, they may choose to pass your book by for something more legible.

Keep contrast in mind. If you have a dark cover image, choose a light font color so that it will stand out.

f. Spine width

You need to calculate the correct spine width for the finished length of your book, which cannot be determined until after the book is properly typeset. Once the number of pages are determined, you need to account for the type of paper used (white or cream).

When you calculate the appropriate width of your book spine, you may use these calculations,

White paper: page count x 0.002252" (0.0572 mm)

Cream paper: page count x 0.0025" (0.0635 mm)

g. Bleed margins

Bleed margins are important if your cover image extends past the printed portion of the page. Make sure you allow for at least 0.125 inches (3.2 mm) to flow past the edges of the finished size. The bleed at the bottom of the page should not exceed this measurement.

h. Cover File Conversion

Before you submit your cover for vetting, you need to convert your native file (.AI, .PSD, etc) to the appropriate file type.

Paperback or hardcover book cover files should be converted to PDF format. If you have specific fonts included, it is best to save the PDF as a flattened image to ensure your fonts are embedded into the file.

Your front cover should be converted to a JPEG file. Make sure you meet the size specifications for the printer you are submitting your file to. Each printer has their own specifications and file size requirements.

As a final check, make sure your front cover file is legible as a thumbnail image. This is often the first image your potential readers see as they look for their next book. If you cannot get a good idea of what your book is about, your readers won't either.

7. Quality Check

Once your manuscript has been typeset, it is best to read your book from the typeset-produced PDF file. This will enable you to check the formatting, as well as read from a file that your readers will experience. It is suggested to read your book aloud.

Make any corrections to the native typeset files and create a new PDF. Make a note of what you changed so that you can duplicate those changes in your eBook files.

This time, go through your PDF file and look for inconsistencies. There should be no headers or footers on blank pages. Does the chapter start on the intended page? Are the headers and footers consistent? Is the overall appearance pleasant?

Make any changes to the native typeset files and produce a new PDF. Do one more check to make sure you caught everything before producing your eBook file.

Check each of your eBook files through various readers. Make sure that you incorporate all the text changes you had made to your typeset files.

The Distribution and Publication Process

This is the exciting part. Months of gestation and preparation have led to this point. Your novel has earned reviews, worthy editorials, endorsements, and hype for its eminent release. Time to make it available to the public.

Add your best endorsements to the back cover of your book. Add any badges you might have won, such as a five-star review from Reader's Favorite.

Check your files one last time to make sure they are error free. You should have the following files,

- Book Cover (PDF)

- Front Cover (JPG)

- Typeset Interior File (PDF)

- Ebook Files (Mobi, EPub)

- Word File (DOC)

Imprint

An imprint is the name of your publisher. The publisher must provide the ISBN number for each book format (paperback, hardback, eBook). If you are publishing the book yourself, you can choose to have your venue produce a free ISBN for you. There are pros and cons for using free ISBN numbers. Without a publisher, you may be limited to where you can distribute your books.

If you want to be your own publisher, you will need to purchase an ISBN from Bowker, as well as a barcode. This can be quite expensive—approximately $150 per ISBN and barcode. You may also choose to purchase a set of 10 numbers and 10 barcodes to save a bit of money.

BookBaby, Amazon, and Smashwords offer free ISBNs under their imprint if you simply want to publish your book and not have to deal with the hassles of becoming a publisher.

Paperback and Hardback Publication and Distribution

There are several on-demand services that will publish your book. Some are free, while others cost a bit of money.

Amazon's CreateSpace (createspace.com) offers free publishing. They also offer some impressive distribution options if you choose to publish only through them. That means that you cannot offer your book through any other service venue, such as Barnes & Nobel. This may limit your ability to reach a broader audience. If you decide to publish your book through multiple services, Amazon will limit your options for distribution.

BookBaby (bookbaby.com) offers a paid publishing service. Depending on how much you want to spend, they can assist you with typesetting, cover design, and marketing strategies. They also offer an impressive distribution service that should satisfy most of your needs.

EBook Publication and Distribution

Amazon and BookBaby also offer eBook services and distribution as part of their publishing process.

Smashwords only produces and distributes electronic books, not printed material. Their service is free and they will distribute your files to every venue that offers electronic books. If you have also published your eBook through Amazon or BookBaby, you will want to limit Smashwords' distribution services to their site only.

Tips on Getting Reviews and Comments

One of the most challenging aspects of writing is promoting your work. Part of promoting is to get people excited about your book. Reviews and comments are an important part of that process.

Some services offer free reviews, while others cost money. It is suggested to try the free route first. Free giveaways are a good way to get reviews and comments. Basically, you offer a free book to a specified number of individuals. You can encourage them to leave a review, but you cannot make it a condition for receiving the free book. To save money, you may like to offer a free ebook instead of a printed copy.

People love sharing their opinions, and many love competitions. Using your preferred social networking avenue, ask people to write a review on Amazon or your vendor of choice. Next, have people vote on the best review. The winners receive a prize (free book, promotional t-shirt, etc.). Make sure you include a deadline.

VistaPrint offers affordable deals on promotional items. I have had great success with pens and shirts. Nothing better than having waitresses and offices use you pens to advertise your books, and people wearing t-shirts that spurs interest in your story.

For top-notch reviews, Kirkus is the cream. They are expensive, however, so be prepared. Readers Favorite, Foreward Reviews, and Library Journal also offer reviews that are worthy of posting on the Editorial section on Amazon.

ReadersFavorite.com offers a free review. Sometimes these can take awhile, but hey, it's free. The reviews are extremely thorough and if you receive five stars, you can place that badge on your website by your book. They also offer an affordable option to purchase three or more reviews that are completed sooner. Upon your approval, the reviews will be posted on Amazon.

Writing blogs is a great way to promote your work. You can either write for your own blog, or contribute to another well-established blog that you respect. If you are lucky, you can get paid for writing blog posts, but most of the time, your only form of payment is promotion.

It is best to promote your book three to six months prior to publishing it. There are several review sites that only review books that are not yet available to the public. Do an internet search for pre-released book reviews and see how many options pop up. Choose a few that best suits your genre and book type.

Get to know other authors in your genre. Ask these authors to write an endorsement that you can include on the back cover of your book. Most of the time, your publisher will have a list of authors who are willing to help you out. Authors stick together—most of the time.

On Amazon, search for books that are similar to the one you wrote and read the reviews. There is an elite group of reviewers who constantly contend to be one of the top reviewers. Click on the name for the reviewer to see if they posted their email address. If so, it is permissible to contact them and ask for a review of your book. Make sure that you tell the reviewer how you found their name and mentioned one or more books they reviewed that are similar to what you wrote.

Rule of thumb: for every 300 people you solicit for reviews, only 100 will actually provide one. It is definitely a numbers game, so plan to be liberal and generous.

When a person comments on your book on social networks or purchasing venues, make sure you respond—kindly. Thank them for their comments. Never respond negatively to any comment, no matter how harsh. People have a right to voice their opinion, but that does not mean their opinion defines who you are. Only you can define your integrity. Keep in mind that some people are just plain mean. Hold your chin up and be proud that you have created something of worth. Never forget that.

About The Authors

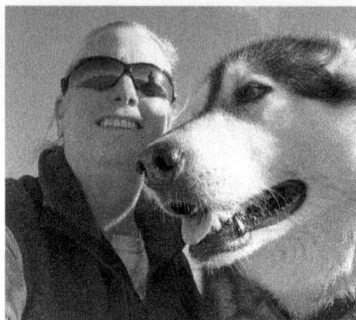

Rowena Portch

With over thirty-three (33) years of professional writing and editing experience, Rowena has worked with small presses across U.S. throughout her career to ensure the publications meet proper cover design and typesetting qualifications.

Rowena is also an award-winning author of ten books and owned and operated a successful publishing business for ten (10) years. She volunteers for Learning Ally as an audio book recording artist and is herself a recording artist for Audible books.

Her academic qualifications include a B.S. in Business Management and an M.S. in Computer Sciences with 16 credits shy of a doctorate in natural medicine.

Sarah Renee Bailey Martin

As an editor and proofreader, Sarah had assisted independent authors and publishers with their manuscripts for the better part of a decade. All of the authors she has worked with have 4.5 to 5 star ratings on Amazon and few have been ranked as USA Today bestsellers.

Sarah also works with Curiosity as their copy editor with the content she corrects getting more than 6 million views every month.

In addition to her work as a proofreader and editor, she is also a reviewer and a content developer. Sarah had assisted companies such as Wainscot Media, Culture Cube and Rooster Grin Media, creating content for clients as small as mom-and-pop stores and as large as major players on Wall Street.

Sarah is an experienced proofreader, editor, reviewer and content developer and has her own site at www.srbmartin.com.